To Esther,

Thank you for reading my Story!

from Sh.kins

To my grandad, Raymond Wild,
Thank you for the creativity!
Love Stephanie
xxx

Published in the United Kingdom by:

Blue Falcon Publishing
The Mill, Pury Hill Business Park,
Alderton Road, Towcester
Northamptonshire, NN12 7LS
Email: books@bluefalconpublishing.co.uk
Web: www.bluefalconpublishing.co.uk

A CIP record of this book is available from the British Library.

First printed 2018
ISBN 978-1912765089

Eleanor Hurl the Peculiar Girl

S L Kins

Eleanor Hurl is a ten year old child
with an imagination that some would call **wild**.

Although to her parents she seems quiet and nice,
her brothers both think that her **hearts** made from ice.

While others have fun baking muffins and cakes,
she'd rather be playing with **spiders** and **snakes**.

Then she'd make poison and chant like the **witches**, scaring her brothers and laughing in stitches!

She's never cared much for dresses and looks –
she'd much rather paint or read **scary** books.
In art class one day, she thought it'd be cool
to terrify the teacher by drawing a ghoul.

And poor Miss Mundy received quite the **fright** - gasping in terror, her face turning white!

She said, "why can't you paint something normal or **pretty**? How about some flowers or a view of the city?"

Eleanor felt herself bubble with **rage**,
this was a masterpiece for a girl of her age!
She threw a huge **tantrum** and fled from the room,
Banished to a corridor of misery and doom.

There she saw something
that struck her with fear,
a large **gruesome** monster
was drawing in near.

She charged at the **creature** to strike it down dead,
Unaware that the big brute would clobber her head.

Whilst she lay wounded and alone on the floor,
a **teacher** came striding down the long corridor.

Eleanor tried to explain what she had just seen.
"There was a monster Miss, it's eyes were **bright green**!"

The teacher started shouting and turned quite unkind.
"These games that you're **playing** are all in your mind.

You're not fighting monsters, you're just a young girl! When will you grow out of this **make-believe** world?"

Sent to **detention** feeling lonely and sad,
Eleanor wondered if her thoughts were all bad.

Then she was approached by young Mr. Hill,
an English teacher who **admired** her skill.

He always said her **imagination** was charming –
although sometimes it could be a little alarming!

"The class could **perform** it at the end of the year;
wouldn't it be nice to see them all cheer?"
So she took out a pencil and wrote down her thoughts,
Delighted that she didn't even have to do sports!

And as Mr. Hill promised, her play was a hit.
No one could believe her **imagination** and wit!
For such a young girl who seemed like a freak,
she proved that there's **talent** in being unique.

List five unique thing about yourself...

1. _____

2. _____

3. _____

4. _____

5. _____

What am I?

"I'm thinking of something rather **scary,**

I'm thinking of something sometimes **hairy.**

I'm thinking of something with many **legs,**

I'm thinking of something that likes **weaving webs.**

Eleanore loves them, **unlike you or me;**

Can you **guess** what the **creature** could be?

Stay original!

Blue Falcon
Publishing

Blue Falcon Publishing is an independent UK publisher, specialising in full-colour picture books.
Our aim is to bring creative stories to engage young children in reading from an early age.
www.bluefalconpublishing.co.uk
email: books@bluefalconpublishing.co.uk
facebook: @bluefalconpublishing

Lightning Source UK Ltd.
Milton Keynes UK
UKHW05f1149111018
330340UK00001B/35/P